Please Y

Please Yourself

Please Yourself

A Celebration

DONALD BISSET

Illustrated by the author

MAMMOTH

James and *The camel who slurped away* first published in *Sleep Tight, Snakey Boo* 1985.
Duck Duck, Gully, Why the ladybird fell downstairs and *Snow Rabbit and the wolves* first published in *The Hedgehog who Rolled Uphill* 1982.
The silent fish first published in *'Oh Dear!' said the Tiger* 1975.
Big Roar and Little Roar first published in *Talks with a Tiger* 1967.
Dogs first published in *Johnny Here and There* 1981.
Yak and *The red hat* first published in *Next Time Stories* 1959.
Fog first published in *Time and Again Stories* 1970.
The lost birthday first published in *Anothertime Stories* 1963.
The death of Ernest first published in *The Joyous Adventures of Snakey Boo* 1982.

First published in Great Britain 1991
by Methuen Children's Books Ltd
Published 1995 by Mammoth
an imprint of Reed Consumer Books Ltd
Michelin House, 81 Fulham Road, London SW3 6RB
and Auckland, Melbourne, Singapore and Toronto

Text and illustrations copyright © 1991 Donald Bisset

ISBN 0 7497 1243 0

A CIP catalogue record for this title
is available from the British Library

Printed and bound in Great Britain
by Cox & Wyman Ltd, Reading, Berkshire

For
Godela von Xylander

The secret of life is never to have an emotion that is unbecoming.

Wilde

Contents

Foreword

Innocence is the essential quality of all Donald Bisset's work – a pure, shining, quite unself-conscious innocence that finds a delighted response in a small child's mind and has an extraordinary *cleansing* effect in an adult's. Of all the writers who protest that they write for only themselves, or the child within them, Bisset is one of the few I would believe. There is genuine simplicity, a total lack of contrivance or artifice or sophisticated humorous hindsight, in his style, plots (if plots there be – perhaps 'sequence of events' is more accurate), characters and dialogue. And yet, at the same time, there is a kind of artless art in the way he looks at words as if they were as new to him as to a four-year-old and follows them with wide-eyed logic to some daft conclusion; in the way he allows his fantasies to develop by the natural laws of free association; in the way he incorporates the very page itself – by the typesetting, the spiky little childlike drawings, the numbering – into the life of the story. The appeal is to the child of around four, five, six, who has learnt just enough of the rules of language, logic, real life, to appreciate seeing them bent, but who still remembers when they were mysterious and unexpected, who is still sufficiently immersed in the world of fairy stories and nursery rhymes to enjoy the comfortable recognition of their patterns, but who has gained enough intellectual distance from them to enjoy also playing with and changing those familiar patterns.

The years – about twenty-five – have scarcely changed Bisset. Perhaps the books tend to be more single units, but they still break up into separate chapter-stories, just a few pages long, bedtime reading at its most engaging. Characters zip in and out of different books: Tiger, who grows fat on words and thrives on a special diet of stories featuring tigers, Komodo the dragon (sometimes papier-mâché, who breathes imaginary fire and dances imaginary polkas, sometimes very old and magical, fuelling a Thames steamboat), and various unnamed but somehow familiar Ducks, Beetles and Snails. The sun, the moon, icebergs, puddles, clouds, rivers, flowers all have their roles to play, but so do quarrelling railway stations, words like Please and Sorry complaining of overwork, lost names whose letters become muddled, chapter headings themselves . . . yet the simple unaffected telling puts paid to hints of whimsy. The sheer effrontery of his little drawings that constantly interrupt the text, and the whole *joie de vivre* that lights up the gentle-hearted world of his imagination, charm storyteller and small listener alike.

Stephanie Nettell

Reprinted from *Twentieth-Century Children's Writers*, 3rd edition, St. James Press, 1989.

Beginning Bit

'What am I about?' said the book – THIS book, to the author. 'I can't see myself, you know! You can see me, but I can't see me. I just AM me. So, please tell me what my stories are about.'

'All right! Some of the stories are about being yourself. Sort of "I'm Me" stories.

'Take *James*, the little tiger in the first chapter. His stripes were lovely but HE didn't like them and felt odd all the time because he looked different from other tigers.

'Look at *Duck Duck* – what a silly duck, pretending that he wasn't even what he was!

'*Hi!* wouldn't do that. *Hi!* is the name of a little boy in a poem in you, Book.'

The book was rather pleased.

'Then there is a story called, *Why the ladybird fell downstairs*. It wasn't sure of itself.

'And *The lost birthday* was found and *Ernest* didn't die. And *Big Roar* roared big roars and *Little Roar* roared little roars. They were happy.

'*Yak* is a sort of philosopher and is very kind.

'*Rabbit and Tiger* – they get in a bit of a muddle. Fancy losing your shadow and having someone else's! They weren't happy till they got their own ones back again. Then they were happy.

'Then there is *Camel* and *Fog* and *The cathedral and the little black cat*. Cat liked being a cat and the cathedral liked being a cathedral and it grew very fond of Cat and Cat grew very fond of the cathedral.

'This book is about life. I like it and I wrote it.

'All that is what your stories are about, Book.'

'Hooray! Thank you. Will you write another book like me, some day?'

'Of course! A bit like you. YOU shall be Volume One and IT shall be Volume Two.'

'Me, Volume One! I like that!'

Read on, dear Reader. Read on!

James

James was a small tiger.
  He looked in the mirror.
  'How strange,' he thought. 'I am not quite right!'
  He went for a walk and met an ox.

  'I am not quite right!' he said.
  The ox looked at him this way.
  Then he looked at him that way.

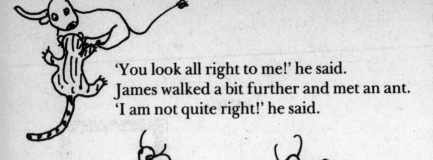

'You look all right to me!' he said.
James walked a bit further and met an ant.
'I am not quite right!' he said.

The ant looked at him this way and looked at him
that way.
'You look all right to me!' he said.
James felt a bit better, but he didn't feel sure.
He met an elephant.

'Am I?' he said.
'Are you what, James?' said the elephant.
'All right?' said James.
The elephant looked at him this way and that way
and then looked and thought.
'Um . . .' said the elephant.
'Er . . .' said the elephant.

20

'Um. Yes. You look fine.'

James was just going to be pleased when the elephant said, 'I think.'

'You think!' said James. 'What do you mean you "think"?'

'Well,' said the elephant. 'You look . . . sort of all right!'

'Sort of?' said James. 'SORT OF? Tigers don't look "sort of" anything. Tigers look ABSOLUTELY BEAUTIFUL. They are yellow. We are yellow with lovely black stripes and green eyes and white whiskers.'

'Yes!' said the elephant, who was embarrassed. 'Yes. Um – well!'

'Well?'

'You look fine!'

'Are you sure?'

'Nearly sure.'

James didn't feel very happy. Then he saw a zebra.

'Ah!' said the elephant. 'Now I see!'

The elephant put one knee on the ground. Then he put his other knee on the ground, then he put his legs somewhere where they couldn't be in the way. Then he lay down and turned on his side.

He looked at James very carefully. 'James!' he said. 'You look a perfectly splendid tiger.'

James purred.

The elephant stood up and looked again. 'Almost,' he said.

James *was* upset.

He lay down to think.

He lay on his side.

'Ah!' said the elephant. 'Now I understand!'

'What?' said James.

The elephant lay on his side and looked again. 'Wrong!' he said.

'What?'

Just then the zebra came up. 'Oh, James!' it said. 'You've got your stripes horizontal; they should be perpendicular!'

James went home.

He looked in his mirror.

He looked at his stripes.

'I've got them on wrong!' he said.

At that moment James's mother came along.

22

'Don't be silly, James!' she said. 'Your stripes are horizontal, like mine.'

James looked at his mother. Then he looked in the mirror.

'Horizontal!' he said.

Then he licked his mother.

'Excuse me!' said a very small voice beside him. It was the ant speaking. 'What does HORIZONTAL mean?'

'This!' said James, pointing to his stripes.

'And what does PERPENDICULAR mean?'

'Perpendicular is when stripes go up – on ordinary tigers like that one over there.'

'Oh!' said the ant, looking at James admiringly. 'I think horizontal stripes are absolutely wonderful!'

'Yes!' said James. He looked in the mirror. He looked at the ordinary tiger. He looked at himself again.

'Yes! Just right!'

He gave the mirror a lick, then went for a walk.

'Just right!' he said.
'Me!'

His mother looked after him.
'Oh, James!' she sighed.

The story of Duck Duck

Once upon a time there was a duck whose name was Duck Duck. Not John Duck or Alfred Duck or Thomas Duck or Mary Duck, but Duck Duck. Duck Duck was a rather timid duck. He said things like, 'Oh dear!' or 'Do you think perhaps I might?' and so on.

One day Duck Duck was wandering along the banks of the stream where he lived when he saw an old mirror leaning against a big log of wood. In fact there was only a little bit of glass left in the mirror, but Duck Duck thought it was a proper mirror and went to have a look at himself in it.

At that moment a pigeon was on the other side of the mirror frame eating some crumbs. Duck Duck went to look at himself and saw the pigeon in what he thought was the mirror.

'Help help!' he cried. 'Quack quack quack! Mummy Mummy Mummy, I'm a pigeon!' He jumped into the stream and paddled frantically towards his mother. 'Mummy, I'm a pigeon. I thought I was a duck. Booohooohooo!' he sobbed, and began to sink.

'Pigeons can't swim!' he thought, and sank deeper and deeper.

'You foolish little duck!' said his mother. 'Of course you're a duck. Go and look in the mirror properly.'

Duck Duck waded ashore and went to look in the mirror.

On the other side of the mirror was a frog.

'A frog!' sobbed Duck Duck. 'Oh, dear me! Mummy, I'm a frog. A heron will swallow me. Oh Mummy! Sob sob sob!'

Mother Duck was quite angry but she thought, 'I must help my silly little son!' So she asked a swan to go and stand behind the mirror frame, then told Duck Duck to go and look at himself.

Duck Duck went very sadly and looked. He could hardly believe his eyes. 'A swan! Oh, I am a foolish duck . . . um . . . er . . . swan. No, I am a wise and beautiful swan!'

He went back to the river and soon became a very boring duck telling the other ducks what to do and being very proud and haughty! He was unbearable. Mother Duck saw that there was nothing behind the mirror frame so she said to Duck Duck, 'Swan, darling, go and look in the mirror.'

'I will!' said Duck. 'I am very handsome.' He swam ashore and went and looked. There was nothing there – except grass and stones and ground. Duck couldn't believe it! He looked and looked. 'Nothing!' he said. 'I'm nothing! I'm not here!' He began to cry. Tears rolled down him and wetted his nice webbed feet. He cried till there was a pool of tears all round him.

He cried some more till the pool was quite deep. He was forlorn. He looked down at the pool and saw what looked like the head and beak of a rather wobbly duck. He kept quite still and the water got quite still and he saw his reflection clearly. He looked and thought and looked and saw. At last he was a sadder and a wiser duck.

He looked at his reflection in the water. He looked in the broken mirror. He looked at the water again. Then he preened his feathers. 'Duck!' he said and preened his feathers some more. He looked again. 'Me!' he said and preened his feathers more still. He looked again. 'Me!' he said. 'Quack quack quack!' Duck liked being Duck.

'Mummy,' he said when he was swimming again, 'I'm me!'

'Of course you are!' said his mother. 'Now go and play with the other ducks!'

'Quack quack quack!' said the other ducks. 'Here comes Duck Duck! Hello, Duck Duck! Come and play!'

'Quack quack quack!' said Duck Duck. 'Quack quack quack quack! Quack quack quack quack! Quack quack quack!'

Hi!

'When I was 1
I'd hardly begun
When I was 2
I hadn't a clue
When I was 3
I began being me
When I was 4
I was me even more
Now I am 5
I am really alive!'

Big Roar and
Little Roar

Once upon a time there was a lion who could only roar little roars. His name was Sam.

'Now go out into the jungle, Sam,' said his mother, 'and roar with the other lions!'

So Sam went into the jungle and all the other lions roared very loudly, 'Roooarr!! Now you roar, Sam,' they said. And Sam went, 'roar roar.'

All the other lions laughed at him. So Sam went home and took some cough mixture to help him roar better. Then he went into the back garden and practised his roaring.

31

But no matter how hard he tried, he could only roar little roars. He did feel sad!

He went into the jungle and met his friend Jack, who was the best roarer in the world.

Jack could roar so loudly that trees trembled when they heard him and clouds scurried away and animals ran and hid. Even the King in his castle was afraid.

'There's Jack roaring again!' he said to the Queen. 'What a noise he makes! I say, my dear, don't you think he'd make a very good guard on the front door, so that no one could come and steal the crown jewels? There's only a cat and a mouse guarding them at the moment.'

'That's a good idea,' said the Queen.

So the King told the Prime Minister to go and ask Jack to come to the castle and guard the crown jewels.

'And ask him to baby-sit, too!' said the Queen. The Prime Minister went into the jungle. When he saw Jack he was afraid and climbed a tree.

'The King says will you please come to the castle and guard the crown jewels?' he said. 'And the Queen says would you please baby-sit, sometimes?'

Jack was very pleased and went to the castle with the Prime Minister. When they got there, the King said, 'Now you sit outside the front gate.'

So Jack roared. 'ROOOAR!! ROOOAR!!'

'That *is* a good roar!' said the King.

But the Queen wasn't pleased.

'Every time he roars he wakes the baby,' she said. 'I will not put up with it.'

She looked out of the window. 'You are very naughty!' she said. 'You roar so loudly you wake the baby.'

Jack thought for a moment. Then he went into the jungle and met his friend Sam, and told him to come to the castle and roar, too.

So Sam came and roared little roars, 'roar roar.'

34

The Queen was very pleased.

'That's very good!' she said. 'When the baby's awake, Jack can be on guard and roar as loud as he likes. And when the baby's asleep Sam can be on guard and roar little roars.'

Sam and Jack were very pleased and danced for joy.

Since the baby was asleep then, Jack went down to the kitchen and the cook gave him his dinner. And Sam stayed on guard and roared little roars, 'roar roar.'

'You *are* a good lion, Sam!' said the Queen.

Why the ladybird fell downstairs

You will notice that this story is not called *HOW* the ladybird fell downstairs or *DID* the ladybird fall downstairs? but *WHY* the ladybird fell downstairs.

A ladybird, strictly speaking, cannot 'accidentally' fall downstairs. It could accidentally fall down *one* stair, but would not then necessarily fall down the next stair. It would have to crawl to the edge first. Crawling is a deliberate action; one does not crawl accidentally.

Of course, ladybirds can *fly* downstairs. So let us rule out 'accident' as a cause.

In my house I have some stairs. And I have a ladybird. It lives in a crack in the wall somewhere. I am not quite sure where.

Anyway, the point about this ladybird is that it falls downstairs every day – before breakfast.

I was intrigued and watched it very carefully.

I noticed that it always fell down seven stairs. Not two or three or nine, always seven. And if I put my ear close to it I could hear it mutter.

Now, I usually have breakfast with my blackbird.

He is a father blackbird with very black feathers and a yellow beak. He has crumbs for breakfast.

I serve them on the windowsill and we chat and look out of the window and discuss the weather or worms or whatever. Also, you understand, I do speak blackbird language, which is a kind of 'tweet-chirp-whistle'. To get the meaning you have to understand the up and down, or rather the upness and the downness, of the whistle part.

Anyway, one morning I told my blackbird about the ladybird. Blackbirds, as a rule, take no notice of ladybirds, at least not socially or snack-wise, so to speak. But my blackbird did know why my ladybird fell downstairs and always seven stairs.

'Tweet-tweet!' said my blackbird. 'It's like this. Ladybirds are red and have seven spots. They are very proud of their spots. Now, I think that the ladybird who lives with you is an anxious ladybird. It's afraid!'

'Afraid?' I said. 'What of?'

'It's afraid that one or more of its spots may drop off.'

'Spots can't drop off. They are part of it!'

'That is true,' said my blackbird. 'Tweet-tweet-whistle! But, while it is true, the ladybird is not quite sure it's true.

'So it crawls to the edge of a stair and then falls off, very carefully, on to one spot. To bang it in. To keep it in place.

'Then it crawls to the next stair and falls on to the next spot, and so on.

'You say it mutters. What does it say?'

'I don't speak ladybird language,' I said, 'but it sounds like, "um bom! uom bomz! uam bomz!"

and so on, and on the last stair it says, "uum bomz!" and then, "coaksostinar".'

'Tweet-tweet!' said my blackbird.

'It is saying,

"one spot!
  two spots!
    three spots!
      four spots!
        five spots!
          six spots!
            seven spots!"
and now for breakfast!'

  'Thank you, my dear!' I said.

  My blackbird finished its crumbs and flew away.

  'What a strange world it is to be sure!' I said.
'Who would have thought that that is why my
ladybird falls downstairs!'

The silent fish

Once upon a time there was a fish named William. He was very very very very clever. He could be silent in ten languages: English, French, Hottentot, Portuguese, Russian, German, Italian, Welsh, Chinese and Swedish. And always, before he was silent in any language, he went, 'Brlp,' and popped a little bubble of air from his mouth to the top of the water.

The other fish *were* impressed. 'Oh, William,' they said, 'please be silent in English.'

'Brlp!' went William and was silent.

Then they said, 'Oh, William, please be silent in French.'

'Brlp!' went William and was silent.

Then they said, 'Oh, William, please be silent in Hottentot.'

'Brlp!' went William and was silent.

'Be silent in Portuguese,' they said.

'Brlp!' went William and was silent. The other fishes *were* pleased.

'Now, William, be silent in Russian,' they said.

'Brlp!' went William and was silent.

'Now, German.'

'Brlp!'

'Now, Italian.'

'Brlp!'

'Oh, William! Now, Welsh. We're sure you can't be silent in Welsh.'

'Brlp!' went William and was silent.

'Now,' said the other fishes, 'dear William, you *are* clever.'

'Brlp!' went William and was silent. 'Brlp! Brlp! Brlp!' He was a very happy fish.

Gully

Gully knew nothing.

He was something, but he didn't know it.

He could feel his hoofs being pulled, but he didn't know it.

He didn't know he had hoofs.

He hadn't been born. Then cold air all round him.

He didn't know it was air. He felt it.

Then a muscle contracted and air rushed inside him.

He breathed.

He was a calf; though he didn't know it.

The darkness was broken up now.

There were shapes but they meant nothing to him.

He could feel something rough and warm rubbing his side.

He felt pleasure.

He waited
    and waited.

'Mooo!' That was something.

'Mooo!' It was his mother, though he didn't know that.

He muzzled something with his lips. Then sucked.
Nothing happened.
He stopped. He was tired.
He lay still, then struggled to stand.
Almost stood.
Fell down.
Went to sleep.
Woke up.
Stood up. Staggered – didn't fall.
Muzzled. Drank. Oh, beauty! Oh, glory!
Paused – looked.
Lightness and darkness. Then there was outside
   and inside.
He ignored outside and inside.
Then fell over.
He thought.
His first ever thought!
A dog barked.
He listened.
His first listen.
He drank.
He fell asleep.
'He's fine!' said the farmer. 'Gully!' he said.
Then to Daisy – 'Good girl.'
Daisy licked Gully.
Gully was a calf.
He'd begun.
When he woke up he stood up.

He butted his mother, half-butted her. Nudged her
   and drank.

'Mooo!' said Daisy.

Dogs

'Wuff wuff!'
    Monday's dog is a disgrace.
He stepped in a puddle and splashed his face.
    He ate some grass and chewed the cud.
Then stood on his head and fell in the mud.
                            'BAD DOG!'

'Wuff wuff!'
    Tuesday's dog has jam for tea
He doesn't like jam but he does like me.
    So he gave me some jam for me to keep
And then pretended to fall asleep.
                            'BAD DOG!'

'Wuff wuff!'
Wednesday's dog is full of woe.
A big fat man stood on his toe.
So he got some milk from a cow in a can
And poured that milk all over the man.
'BAD DOG!'

'Wuff wuff!'
Thursday's dog is no good at singing.
So he borrowed a hat and barked for a living.
He barked all day, then barked all night,
He couldn't sing but he barked all right.
'BAD DOG!'

'Wuff wuff!'

Friday's dog painted some spots.

Some were big and some were dots.

To pretend he'd got measles, and should stay in bed.

'I've got measles,' was what he said.

'BAD DOG!'

'Wuff wuff!'

Saturday's dog howled for his mum.

He howled and howled but his mum couldn't come.

So he barked at butterflies and ate brown bread,

And twice a day he fell down dead.

'POOR DOG!'

'Wuff wuff!'
    Sunday's dog is as good as gold.
Doesn't pull on his lead and 'sits' when he's told.
    He likes the postman and sits on the mat,
Then brings in the letters and kisses the cat.
                'GOOD DOG!'

The red hat

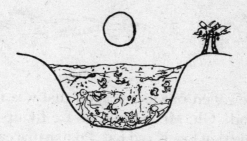

Once upon a time there was a little fish swimming in the sea with a lot of other little fishes.

All down below him the water looked dark and the deeper he went the darker it got. But when he looked up he could see the blue sky and a red hat. 'I would like that red hat,' he thought.

So he said goodbye to the other fishes and swam up and up and up till he got to the top of the water and all around him was the sea and big ships and above him was the blue sky and large white clouds and the red hat.

He tried to swim higher but no matter how hard he tried he couldn't get higher than the top of the water.

So he called out to a seagull that was flying just overhead. 'Oh, Mr Seagull, please fly up high and bring me that lovely red hat. I'd like to wear it.'

But the seagull said, 'You'd better go away, little fish, or I'll eat you for my breakfast.' And he dived down at the little fish and tried to catch him in his big sharp yellow beak, but the little fish swam under the water and got away.

Then he saw a fisherman in a boat with a great long fishing line with a hook on the end of it. So he looked out of the water and he said, 'Oh please, Mr Fisherman, will you try and catch that red hat in the sky for me with your long line and hook?'

'You'd better look out,' said the fisherman, 'or I'll catch YOU!' And he twirled the fishing line round his head three times and sent the hook spinning towards the little fish, but he just missed him and the little fish swam away.

A little while later the little fish came to a river and there on the bank he saw an elephant who was singing a little song to himself:

'The elephant is large and fat
He eats so much of this and that.
He likes to sit and gorge and cram
On hay and grass and strawberry jam.'

The little fish called out, 'Will you please stretch out your long trunk and fetch me down that red hat from the sky?'

So the elephant stretched out his trunk as far as he could.

He stretched and he stretched but he couldn't reach the red hat. 'I'll tell you what I'll do,' he said. 'I'll pick you up in my trunk and I'll twirl you around and throw you as high as I can right up in the sky and you can fetch down the hat for yourself.'

So he picked up the little fish and threw him high up into the air, higher than the clouds, right up into the blue sky, and the little fish looked and he saw that it wasn't a red hat in the sky but the sun.

Then he fell right back into the sea with the biggest splash you've ever seen.

All the other little fishes swam round him and said, 'Why haven't you brought back the red hat?'

'It isn't a red hat,' he told them. 'It's the sun.' And they all laughed at him.

'Don't be silly,' they said. 'Of course it's a red hat.'
And they swam away to play games.

Yak

Far, far away from anywhere, in the mountains of Tibet, there lived a Yak.

Of course he wasn't really far from anywhere. He was near the snow and the ice and the sleet and the cold wind and wet grass and craggy rocks. All day the blizzard howled and the sun was hidden behind clouds. And the black crows flew about in the storm-tossed air. Yes, he was near all that. But he was far away from the shops and picture books and ice creams and telly and children going to school.

Now the Yak hadn't got a name, so I will just call him Yak.

Well, Yak was very fond of sitting in a fairly quiet part behind some rocks and listening to the sound of the sea. He had found a seashell, a lovely spiral seashell, and when he held his ear to it he could hear the sea.

Goodness knows how it had got there, but there it was – and it was what Yak liked best in the world. He usually hid the shell from the other yaks and the crows during the daytime, but at night when the stars were out, he would sit behind the rocks on the mountain and listen to the sound of the sea in his shell. And he was filled with a great longing to go to the seaside. So, one day, he picked up his spiral shell, said goodbye to the other yaks and set off. You might wonder how a yak carries a spiral shell when he is walking. If you look at the picture you will see he carried it on one of his horns.

He didn't know which way to go but he thought, 'I'll just keep on walking till I get to the sea.' So he walked all day and in the evening he ate some grass and listened to the sea in his shell and went to sleep. He walked all the next day and the next but still he didn't come to the sea.

All round him were the mountains. Sometimes he saw a herd of llamas and once he saw an eagle flying high up in the air, but he never seemed to get nearer the sea.

One day he was drinking from a little mountain stream and feeling rather sad. He sat down beside it and took down his shell and listened.

The stream was running babbling over stones, and it looked at Yak and wondered what he was doing. So it asked him, 'What are you doing?'

'I'm listening,' said Yak.

'Oh, let me listen too,' said the stream.

Yak held the shell near the stream and the stream listened. 'Why, that's the sea!' it said. 'That's the sea!'

'Do you know the way there?' asked Yak.

'Do I know the way!' replied the stream. 'Why, I'm going there all the time. Just you follow me and you'll get there.'

'Thank you,' said Yak, and he followed it.

Presently the stream grew bigger until at last it was a broad river with boats sailing on it. 'It would be nice to sail in a boat instead of having to walk,' thought Yak. So he got in a boat and paid his fare and away they went.

The boat had a big red sail and the wind blew it along while Yak just sat and had a nice rest.

At last they got to the seaside. It was wonderful. He sat down on the sand and watched the waves come in. They sounded exactly like they did in his seashell.

Yak was very happy. 'This is nicer than the wet, cold mountains,' he thought.

He found a cave to sleep in at night.

It was very nice there. He liked the seaside, but best of all were the late evenings when it was growing dark and the people had gone home, and Yak sat by himself outside his cave and listened to the sound of the sea and watched the ships passing in the distance and the sun set on the horizon; and then, in the dark, the stars coming out one by one, and the waves lapping on the shore.

The hedge

Once there was a hedge. It was lonely because all the other hedges had been cut down.

'I wouldn't mind,' thought the hedge, 'if only some small animal would come along and live among all my leaves and prickles.'

There was a colony of sparrows living in its top branches. 'But sparrows don't count,' thought the hedge. 'They've no conversation. They just chitter and chatter among themselves all day long. And they are very quarrelsome.

Just then an elephant came along.

'Oh, this is a ridiculous story!' thought the hedge. 'Fancy an elephant coming along!'

'Hello, Hedge!' said the elephant.

'Hello, Elephant,' said the hedge. 'You can't come and live in my prickles. You're much too big.'

'I wasn't thinking of that,' said the elephant. 'I was thinking of eating you.'

'Me?' said the hedge. 'By my roots and prickles. I've never heard of anything so stupid.'

'I'm hungry,' said the elephant.

'Do you like marmalade?' said the hedge.

'No!' said the elephant.

'Well, I taste of marmalade,' said the hedge.

'Oh,' said the elephant. 'Well, haha, goodbye then.'

'The very idea!' said the hedge to itself.

It saw some huntsmen coming towards it.

'Have you seen a fox coming this way?' asked the Master. 'We're trying to catch it.'

'It wasn't a fox,' said the hedge, 'it was an elephant.'

'Tut tut!' said the Master. He blew his horn and rode off with all the other huntsmen.

When they had gone the hedge said, 'You can come out now, Foxy. I knew you were there. You are quite safe now.'

'Was there really an elephant here?' asked the fox.

'Oh, yes!' said the hedge. 'It didn't like marmalade. Would you like to live in my leaves and branches and prickles, Foxy?' Then the hedge thought, 'A fox would be such good company.'

'Would you like to stay with me?'

'I've got a wife and three children,' replied the fox. 'My home's very comfortable. Four rooms and running water nearby. I don't think my wife would like to come and live among your leaves and branches and prickles. Especially the prickles! Goodbye.'

'Oh dear!' said the hedge. 'Oh dear! Oh dear!'

Just then it saw a very prickly animal indeed.

'Hello,' said the prickly animal. 'I'm looking for a nice house to live in. All the other animals have got nice houses. Badger has got a house under the roots of a tree in the forest. Owl has got a hole in an oak tree and Rabbit has got a burrow. And Snail has got a small house of his own on his back. But I haven't got a house. I am a sad hedgehog.'

'What?' said the hedge. 'Say that again.'

'I haven't got a house.'

'No – the other part, after you said you were sad.'

'A sad hedgehog,' said the hedgehog.

'Oh, bliss!' said the hedge. 'A hedgehog. Oh, bliss and double bliss. A hedgehog – a hedgehog.' It was an excited hedge.

Well, let us make no more ado, and say that they lived happily together ever after.

'I like it here!' said the hedgehog.

Fog

Once upon a time, on the Queen's birthday, the fog had come to London to see the Trooping of the Colour. But when it got there the Queen said to the General, 'We won't have the Trooping of the Colour today because it's foggy.'

And this happened every time the fog came. So it felt sad. It did want to see the Trooping of the Colour. But how could it, if every time it came to London the Queen said, 'Cancel the Parade'?

Now, at Buckingham Palace, under the Queen's chair, there lived a cat, whose name was Smokey, and he felt very sorry for the fog and wanted to help it. So, next year, just before the Queen's birthday, he wrote a letter.

UNDER THE QUEEN'S CHAIR
THE PALACE
   TUESDAY
DEAR FOG,
    PLEASE COME TO THE PALACE
      YOURS SINCERELY
        SMOKEY

That night, before she went to bed, the Queen put the cat out of the back door of Buckingham Palace and went upstairs to bed.

And, sure enough, before Smokey had time to miaow three times, he saw the fog. They were pleased to see each other.

'I do want to see the Trooping of the Colour,' said the fog. 'But they always cancel the parade when it's foggy so I never get to see it.'

'I know,' said Smokey. 'Now, tomorrow you must arrive just as the soldiers are going on parade and when the General sees you he'll say, "Your Majesty, there's a fog. Shall I cancel the parade?"'

'Yes, he always says that,' said the fog with a sigh.

'Then,' continued Smokey, 'just as the Queen is going to say, "Yes, cancel the parade!", you miaow.'

'All right!' said the fog. 'But how do I miaow?'

So Smokey showed him and the fog practised till it was good at miaowing.

Next morning the soldiers were all lined up for the parade when the General said, 'Shall I cancel the parade, Your Majesty? I see a fog.'

'Where?' said the Queen.

'There!' said the General, pointing to the fog.

Just then the fog miaowed.

'Really, General,' said the Queen. 'Can't you tell the fog from a pussy cat? I distinctly heard it miaow. Of course you can't cancel the parade!'

So the fog stayed and saw the Trooping of the Colour after all. It felt happy now and went away to live on top of the mountains in Wales, where there were other fogs to play with.

Once the Queen wrote to it:

And the fog wrote back:

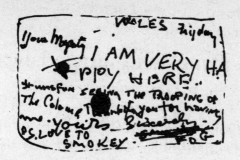

The Queen can't understand it. 'How did the fog manage to see the Trooping of the Colour, Smokey?' she asks him, looking under her chair.

But Smokey just purrs. That's his secret.

The camel who slurped away

In a quiet part of the desert in Africa, a few miles south of the pyramids, there lived a man whose name was Abdul.

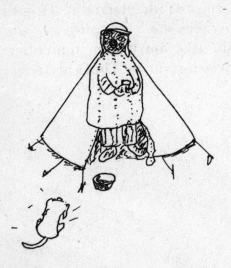

One day he stood outside his tent with an empty glass in his hand and said to his dog, 'Neptune, please guard my tent while I go to get a glass of water.'

'Woof!' said Neptune. 'Woof, woof, woof!' Which meant, 'Yes, Master, I will do that. Woof, woof, woof! I will sit and eat my bone until you come back.' Abdul trudged off and at last he came to a tap.

'Hello, Tap,' he said.

'Gurgle!' said the tap. 'Hello, Abdul.'

'I've come for a glass of water,' said Abdul. He filled his glass and was just going to drink when he felt a tickle on his cheek. He looked round – nothing there. He went to take a drink but his glass was empty. 'Strange,' he thought. 'I am sure I filled it.' He filled it again. He felt a tickle on his other cheek. 'What's that?' he thought, and turned — nothing there!

He turned back and put his glass to his lips and drank some nothing, because it hadn't got anything in it.

'This,' said Abdul to himself, 'is ridiculous! However . . .' He filled the glass again. He looked at it very carefully. It was full of water. 'Delicious!' he said. Then he heard a cough behind him. He turned round quickly – nothing! Abdul couldn't believe it. 'I distinctly heard a cough!' said Abdul and went to take a drink. The glass was empty. Abdul turned round and round and round – no one there! He bent down and looked between his legs. He could see the material of his robe.

'Oh, that's me!' he said. 'Silly me!' He pulled his robe up and looked again.

'Nothing there!' he said. 'Only my feet and four other feet. Other feet??!!'

He poured another drink and heard a little cough behind him. He looked round and back as quickly as he could.

A camel was there drinking.

'So it was you?' said Abdul. 'Tickling my cheek and then coughing behind me as I turned round.'

The camel nodded and pointed to his hump with his left fore-foot. Abdul understood and gave the camel a hundred glasses of water to drink. It took nearly two hours but it did fill the camel's hump.

The camel was very pleased and kissed Abdul goodbye and slurped away. Abdul watched it.

Slurp slurp slurp! it went. It was very full of water, which slurped as it moved.

The story of the cathedral
and the little black cat

'Good morning, Little Black Cat' said the Cathedral.

'Miaow!' said the little black cat. 'Can I scratch my back against that little arch of yours? I've got a tickle!'

'Of course,' said the Cathedral. 'Go ahead.'

The little black cat's name was Samuel, by the way. I think I'll call him Sam.

Sam rubbed his back. Oooooooooo! It was lovely. He wandered inside and looked round. 'Miaow!' he said. 'You *are* big. A million cats could get in here.'

'And leave room for a million more,' said the Cathedral. 'You'd have to stack them, of course.'

Sam thought, 'How do you stack cats? They wouldn't stack, I'm sure. They'd all say "Miaow!" and jump down.'

The Cathedral was very beautiful. There were a hundred tall candles inside, flickering brightly.

'Cathedral,' said Sam, 'what are cathedrals for?'

'Tell me first,' said the Cathedral, 'what are little black cats for?'

'For people to stroke,' said Sam, 'and to listen to us purring. Cats are very good for children. Especially babies. They like each other.'

'That is very good,' said the Cathedral. 'I am sure God cares for little black cats as well as for people.'

Sam was a bit puzzled. 'Who is God?' he said. 'Is he a "he" or a "she" or an "it"?'

'All of them,' said the Cathedral.

'Where does God live?' Sam asked.

'Here, there and everywhere.'

'In the sky?'

'There too!'

'Why doesn't he fall down?'

The Cathedral sighed and looked at the little black cat. 'God is inside your head.'

'Is he inside my tail, too?'

'If you think with your tail, he is,' said the Cathedral.

'Oh!'

'Now, I'll tell you what cathedrals are for. They are a special place for people to come and say their prayers.'

'Can cats say their prayers too?'

'Yes.'

'I will say my prayers now,' thought Sam.

'Miaow miaow miaow mew miaw!'

'Miaow! – I've just prayed.'

'Did God answer?'

'Yes,' said Sam, sadly.

'What did he say?'

'He said, "Myeow myrrgh, miaow miaow miaw miaow!"'

'Of course,' said the Cathedral. 'God speaks in cat language to cats. And in dog language to dogs and in clickety clickety click insect language to beetles. What did he say in "people" language?'

'Well,' said Sam, 'I prayed that I could catch the pigeon in the courtyard outside. And he answered that the pigeon had already prayed not to be caught by a little black cat.'

'Oh dear. You can't have a pigeon who is caught and not caught, can you?' said the Cathedral, sympathetically.

Sam wandered out again. But just then a policeman with his Alsatian came along. It was a big dog and barked at Sam.

Sam sprang up on to an arch and from there to a higher one, and from there to a higher one still.

The dog went on barking.

Sam did not arch his back and bristle his hair and put out his claws. He knew he was safe, so he just sat and ignored the dog, who barked a bit more and then went away.

Sam looked at the Cathedral through a little archway.

It looked beautiful.

The candles flickered.

Then Sam saw a notice, just outside the Cathedral entrance, which said: NO DOGS ALLOWED.

Sam went inside the Cathedral, through the little hole that was the archway, and slipped inside, purring.

The lost birthday

Once upon a time there was a big father elephant who lived at Whipsnade Zoo with a mother elephant and their little elephant, whose name was Yalmar.

Father elephant was very, very big. Mother elephant was quite big. And even Yalmar wasn't *very* little. Elephants aren't!

One day they saw the father elephant standing on his head.

'Whatever are you doing?' said the mother elephant.

'I'm trying to remember something!' said the father elephant.

'What are you trying to remember?'

'If I knew that,' said the father elephant, 'I wouldn't be trying to remember it, my dear, would I?' and he walked off.

'Now, run along, Yalmar,' said the mother elephant, 'and see if you can find what your father's forgotten.' Yalmar ambled off by himself. After a while he climbed a little hill by a bamboo wood and sat down and watched the clouds chasing each other across the sky.

Presently he heard the sound of crying. He couldn't see anything but the crying seemed to come from quite near. So he said, 'Please don't cry. I'll help you.'

78

The crying stopped.

'Who are you?' said Yalmar. 'I can't see you.'

'I'm a lost birthday,' said a voice, 'and I don't know who I belong to.'

'Oh dear!' said Yalmar. 'That is sad. And is there a birthday cake, too?'

'Of course. There's always a birthday cake on birthdays,' said the lost birthday. 'This one's got six candles. Someone's six today.'

'How nice to be six,' thought Yalmar. 'That's a very nice age. Almost as nice as being seven. Five is nice, too, and so is four. And as for eight, well, when you're eight you're nearly halfway to being grown up. Still, I think I'd like being six best. I'm terribly sorry, though, I can't help you. I don't know who's forgotten a birthday.'

Yalmar started off home. When he got there his father had stopped standing on his head and was eating some hay.

'I remembered,' he said. 'I knew it was yesterday or tomorrow or perhaps today. And it is!'

'It is what?' asked Yalmar.

'Your birthday,' said his mother, coming in. 'You're six today.'

Yalmar *was* excited. He trundled off as quickly as he could to the little hill by the bamboo wood.

'Hello!' he called out. 'You're MY birthday. I'm six today.'

'Hooray!' said the birthday. 'Hooray hooray hooray!'

That afternoon, at tea-time, Yalmar had a birthday cake with six candles and he curled his trunk round and *blew* all the candles out at once.

'It is fun!' he thought. 'I like being six.'

Snow Rabbit and the wolves

It had been snowing all night. The sun rose from behind a little hill and cast long shadows on the ground.

Suddenly Snow Rabbit appeared in the distance, jumping along, scattering snow all round him. Snow Rabbit was feeling better. He had been a humble rabbit for two whole days and now was his old arrogant self again.

'Lollipop! Lollipop! I'm a snow rabbit. Lollipop! Lollipop! Jump!'

Nearly every time that Snow Rabbit jumped he jumped a little higher than the last time. He wanted to lose his shadow. He was a white snow rabbit and the ground that morning was white with snow. 'If it wasn't for my shadow and my little grey nose I'd be invisible,' he thought. He jumped higher, but every time he landed his shadow returned to him. He was so busy watching his shadow that he didn't see Tiger till he was almost on top of him, nor did he hear Snow Owl coming up behind him, and Snow Owl was so intent on catching Snow Rabbit that he didn't see Tiger either.

Tiger sprang up – too late!

Their shadows jumped and sprang too, and got all mixed up so that you couldn't tell which was which.

Rabbit raced away and Tiger's shadow got in a muddle and came with him: Jumpety! Jumpety! Jumpety! Jumpety! Jumpety!

Rabbit's shadow stayed with Tiger. Tiger looked at his new shadow and thought, 'Oh dear! I've changed into a snow rabbit, and here comes a snow owl who will eat me for his dinner.' He bounded off as fast as he could. Bound! Bound! Bound! And Snow Rabbit's shadow bounded with him.

Snow Owl was quite unused to this sort of thing and felt confused.

He looked down to make sure his own shadow was with him on the ground. Then he flew home, supperless, to bed in the hole in the tree trunk where he lived.

Snow Rabbit was going along, Jumpety! Jumpety! when he saw three wolves. He saw their noses and their tails. They were hiding behind some bushes. He was just going to run away when he caught sight of his tiger shadow beside him. He suddenly felt very brave and strong. 'Huh!' he thought. 'Why should I be afraid of wolves? I'LL CHASE THEM!' He went straight for them. Jumpetyjumpetyjumpety! The wolves *were* surprised.

'Look at that terrible rabbit!' said the first wolf.

'Ferocious!!!' said the second wolf.

'I want my mummy!' said the third wolf, and howled.

Snow Rabbit got nearer and nearer. The wolves' hair stood on end with fright. Then they all turned and ran. They ran so fast that they were soon out of sight.

Presently they saw Tiger. He was bounding along with very little bounds: bnd bnd bnd bnd!

'Hey!' said the first wolf, stopping.

'What?' said the second wolf, stopping.

'It looks like . . .' said the third wolf – 'A TIGER!!' said all the wolves.

They hid and watched. It seemed a strange sort of tiger. As he passed them, a little way off, a sparrow flew out of a hedge near him. Tiger started and cringed a bit!

'It's a timid tiger,' said the first wolf.

'It looks as if it wouldn't say boo to a goose,' said the second wolf.

'Look! There *is* a goose,' said the third wolf.

'Honk honk!' said the goose. Tiger slunk off and hid behind a tree.

'Come on,' said the first wolf. 'Let's chase it.'

They did. The goose flew off, honking loudly.

Tiger saw the wolves. Did he roar? No!

Did he snarl? No!

Did he lash his tail and make his sharp claws stick out? No! Did he run away? Yes, he did!

He ran
  and ran
    and ran
      and he ran – till the wolves were far away.

Tiger ran about two miles. Snow Rabbit ran about two miles. Tiger had run that way.

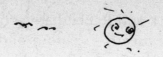

And Rabbit had run that way.

The wolves had given up and gone home.

Tiger approached the hedge from one direction and bounded over it. Snow Rabbit approached the hedge from the opposite direction and bounded over it, too.

They met in mid-air. Bang!!

Oh, what a scuffle there was!

Which was Tiger?

Which was Rabbit?

There . . . there . . . there . . . this way . . . that way . . . upside down . . .

'Whew!!!'

Then they stopped and looked at each other. But in the scuffle where they had whirled about like clothes in a spin dryer, Rabbit's shadow, who had been with Tiger, and Tiger's shadow, who had been with Rabbit, got mixed up. Tiger had *his* own shadow back and Rabbit had *his* own shadow. They were out of breath – shadows and all! Tiger looked at Rabbit and thought, 'It would be fun playing with Rabbit.' Snow Rabbit looked at Tiger. 'He *is* big,' he thought. 'And he's very here and there and everywhere at once. Um . . . I suppose I had better run away. But I wish we were friends.' Snow Rabbit turned to run.

Tiger, quick as a flash, put his paw on top of him. But he didn't unsheathe his claws. 'Snow Rabbit,' he said. 'You're a sportsman.'

'Tiger?' said Snow Rabbit.

'Sorry!' said Tiger. 'Don't run away, little rabbit.'

Snow Rabbit didn't run away. They played. They had a lovely time. Sometimes Rabbit hid and Tiger counted ten then tried to find him. And Tiger hid – although he was big he was difficult to find. He didn't need to hide much. He just stood quite still, and the patterns of sunlight through leaves and long grass matched his stripes.

When Snow Rabbit got very near, Tiger went 'ROARRRR!!!!'

Which made Snow Rabbit jump higher than he ever had jumped before.

The death of Ernest
(A story for Snakey Boo)

'How is it with you, Big Snake?' said Asp coming up.

'I am in the mood for a story, slithery, slithery Asp,' said Snakey Boo.

'I am dry. I am sandy and wriggly, not slithery,' said Asp. 'Would you like *me* to tell you a story?'

'Yes, please!' said Snakey Boo. 'Tell me a sad story.'

'How sad?'

'Very very sad.'

'Once upon a time,' said the asp, 'there was a beetle whose name was Ernest. From his front nose to his back legs . . .'

'Did he have two noses?'

'No, just one in front.'

'How many legs?'

'Six.'

'Thank you.'

'Ernest was a quarter of a millimetre long from his nose to his back legs. He was smaller than the smallest pinhead in the world. But he was a very proud beetle. He was proud because he was very good at humming. He thought, "I am the best hummer in the world!"

'One day his mother said to him, "I am just going out for a crawl to the shops. Please be a good boy and stay at home till I come back."

"'I will!" said Ernest.

"'Promise?"

"'I promise!" said Ernest – and he meant it.

'He was quite happy at home and practised his humming. He hummed, "Hmmmmmmmmmmm-mmmmmmmmmmmmmmmmmmmmmmmmmmm-mmmmmmmmmmm!"

'He hummed some more.

"Hmmmmmmmmmmmmmmmmmmmmmmmmmm-mmmmmmmmmmmmmmmmmmmmmmm!"

'He *was* pleased. Then, from somewhere, he heard,

"HMMMMMMMMMMMMMMMMMMMM-MMMMMMMMMMMMMMMMMMMMMMMMMM-MMMMMMMMMMMMMMMMMMMMMMMMMM-MMMMMMMMMMMMMMM!!!"

'It was a wonderful hum! You would have thought that Ernest would have been pleased to hear it. But not a bit of it! He was jealous. The humming went on, "HMMMMMMMMMMMMM-MMMMMMMMMMMMMMMMMMMMMMMMMM-MMMMMMMMMMMMMMMMMMMMMMMMMM-MMMMMMMMMMMMMMMMMMMMMMMMMM-MMMMMMMMMMMMMMMM!!!"

'It was his mother's new refrigerator. It loved humming, too, sometimes – just like yours and mine does.

'Ernest was furious. He forgot his promise and put his hat on and went out and crawled along the world.'

'Where?' said Snakey Boo.

'The world! On top of it, where the ground is.'

'Whereabouts?'

'Salisbury Plain,' said Asp. 'Now listen, Snakey, and don't ask so many questions.'

'Well, there was Ernest being very naughty and in a bad temper and crawling along Salisbury Plain. And in the sky – somewhere in all the sky a snowflake was waiting to fall. Then it started to fall!

'Just one snowflake?'

'Yes.'

'Just one?'

'Just one! It floated down, faster and faster till it came to Salisbury Plain.

'Down
  and down
   and down
     and DOWN – LIKE AN
        AVALANCHE – right on top of Ernest.'
'Is that the end?'
'Yes!'
'Sad!'
'A tragedy! A tragedy!'
'Asp?'
'Yes?'
'Thank you! I liked your story.'
'Any time,' said Asp and wriggled away.

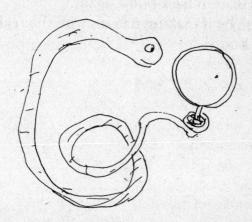

Then Snakey saw something very, very small moving along. It hopped. Then it hopped again – and again.

'It's not a beetle,' thought Snakey Boo. 'It's not a grasshopper or, for that matter, a kangaroo. Oh, I am a silly snake.'

He got out his magnifying glass and looked again. 'You're a flea!' said Snakey Boo.

The flea nodded. 'My name is Sparticus,' she said. 'Julia Sparticus Flea. I've come to be a flea in this storybook.'

'Welcome!' said Snakey Boo. Then he sighed. 'Poor Ernest.'

'Oh, no!' said Julia Sparticus. 'He hid under a daisy. He loved the snowflake. He drank it.'

'So he didn't die?'

'No. He went back home again.'

'I hope he is making friends with the fridge!' said Snakey Boo.